Simon and the snowflakes

Gilles Tibo

Tundra Books

My name is Simon and I love to count.

When the first snow begins to fall,
I run out to count the flakes.

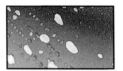

But the flakes come down too fast.

How can I ever count them?

If I count the flakes that fall on a bird
And then count all the birds,
I will know how much snow falls.

I stand on a tree trunk with my broom.
But the birds fly by too fast.

I go to a field to ask the snowman:
"How many flakes are there in a snowfall?"

"That's easy, Simon," said the snowman.
"There's a snowflake for every star in the sky."

I go up a hill to count the stars.

My friend Marlene brings a ladder.
We pull down stars and count them.
We fill our toboggan with stars.

But the stars move away across the sky.

I stand on a snowbank to ask the moon:
"How many stars are there in the sky?"

"That's easy, Simon," said the moon.
"As many lights as there are in a city."

I get on my sled and ride to the city.

I go up a mountain to count the lights.

But the lights go on and off.

I go to the forest to meet my friends.

I cannot count the lights in a city,
the stars in the sky,
the flakes in a snowfall.

But some things I can count.

To Danielle and Marlène

© 1988, Gilles Tibo
Published in Canada by Tundra Books, Montreal, Quebec H3G 1R4
Published in the United States by Tundra Books of Northern New York, Plattsburgh, NY 12901
Distributed in the United Kingdom by Ragged Bears Ltd., Andover, Hampshire SP11 9HX

ISBN 0-88776-218-2 (hardcover)   ISBN 0-88776-274-3 (paperback)
Library of Congress Catalog Card Number 88-50258

Also available in a French edition, *Simon et les flocons de neige* :
ISBN 0-88776-219-0 (hardcover)   ISBN 0-88776-275-1 (paperback)
Library of Congress Catalog Card Number 88-50259

Canadian Cataloguing in Publication Data: Tibo, Gilles, 1951–. Simon and the snowflakes. I. Title. PS8589.I26S44 1988 jC843'.54
C88-090132-2 PQ3919.2.T43S44 1988

3ROCKWOO11799G

Printed in Hong Kong by South China Printing Co (1988) Limited.